GREAT ILLUSTRATED CLASSICS

THE COUNT OF MONTE CRISTO

Alexandre Dumas

**adapted by
Mitsu Yamamoto**

**Illustrations by
Pablo Marcos Studio**

**BARONET
BOOKS**

BARONET BOOKS, New York, New York

GREAT ILLUSTRATED CLASSICS

**edited by
Malvina G. Vogel**

Contents

About the Author

Alexandre Dumas was born in a small town in France in 1802. His father was a general and a companion of Napoleon. Later Dumas used Napoleon and his friends as characters in his novels. Dumas grew up to be a huge man like his father. He loved to eat, spend money, be with friends—and write.

He went to Paris and wrote plays. They were a success. When he turned to novels, they were an even greater success. He combined real people and events from French history with imagined people and plots. Soon he was forced to hire writers to help him get down on paper all the stories he was bursting with. Even though critics called this a "Fiction Factory," Dumas produced hundreds of books, all widely read.

The most famous of all Dumas' books are *The Three Musketeers, The Man in the Iron Mask,* and *The Count of Monte Cristo.* They have been read for over 100 years and made into movies several times.

The Count of Monte Cristo has two themes which were Dumas' favorites—revenge and money. He often dreamed of revenge against the critics who attacked him. And he loved money, so the thought of the Count's unlimited wealth excited him. Dumas, himself, became rich from his writings, but he spent so freely that he died penniless in 1870.

Parts of the *The Count of Monte Cristo* may seem unbelievable. Even so, the reader enjoys the excitement and the speed at which the story moves. Most of all, the reader wants the Count to triumph—and he does!

The *Pharaon* Comes Home.

CHAPTER 1

The Ship Without a Captain

A little boy first sighted the masts of the ship *Pharaon*. She was coming home to Marseilles, France, with a cargo of cloth and dyes. As usual, a crowd gathered to watch the docking, an exciting event in 1815, for the handling of big sailing ships was an art. But the *Pharaon* proceeded toward port so slowly that the onlookers felt something must be wrong on board.

Monsieur Morrel, the owner, was overjoyed to hear that his ship was home. Now he saw that a tall sailor stood beside the wheel where old Captain Leclere should have been. Morrel ordered a rowboat. He wanted to know the bad news at once. As he neared the *Pharaon*, he saw she was under the command of Edmond Dantes.

Edmond ordered a rope dropped, and his employer climbed aboard. He looked anxiously into Edmond's dark, intelligent eyes that now were full of sympathy.

"Bad news, sir. Captain Leclere is dead and buried at sea. He came down with brain fever after we left Naples, Italy. He was raving toward the end, so I gave the crew orders from then on. Your cargo and ship are safe and sound."

Morrel heard this news with many changes of expression. Though his captain was dead, before him stood a fine replacement. Edmond Dantes was tall and strong and knew the sea. His handsome face was sunburned from many voyages, though he was only nineteen.

A Worried Owner Goes Aboard.

Morrel shook Edmond's hand and thanked him. "I must consult my partner, but I think he will agree with me that the new captain of the *Pharaon* will be you."

Edmond's face lit up with happiness. "I hoped, sir, that I might have a chance. The crew and I are like brothers. Not one resents my youth and . . . . "

Edmond stopped and his face clouded. He was watching a man who had come from below and was now walking toward them. The newcomer was a grim-faced man about twenty-six. This was Monsieur Danglars. Edmond corrected his last statement. "There may be one who is not like my brother. Please excuse me, sir, I must give orders to drop anchor and dock the ship."

Danglars greeted his employer with a great show of respect. He glanced around to see that no one else was listening before he said, "Monsieur Morrel, I must report the

The New Captain of the *Pharaon*

mishandling of the *Pharaon*. No sooner was our wonderful captain dead when this Dantes seized command. Then he lost us time by putting into the island of Elba for no reason. The ship needed no repairs. Perhaps he merely wished to have a stroll ashore after being so long at sea. He is very young, you know."

Morrel frowned. "That was very wrong. But, as for taking command, he had that right as First Mate, Danglars. It was good experience since he will be the new captain, if my partner agrees with me."

Danglars' grim face concealed his disappointment at these words. He wanted to be made captain himself, mainly because of the increase in salary that went with it.

When Morrel questioned Edmond about the stop at Elba, he found the young man's answer satisfactory. Just before Captain Leclere began raving from his fever, he had ordered the stop. Edmond was to report to Napoleon in

Danglars Wants to Be Captain.

Leclere's place and obey any orders the ex-Emperor of France gave.

When Morrel heard Napoleon mentioned, he looked around uneasily. Napoleon had been stripped of his powers and now lived in exile on Elba. But there were many Frenchmen who worked in secret to restore him to the throne. Morrel was a businessman and did not involve himself in politics. So he asked no further questions about the visit to Elba and cautioned Edmond not to mention it to anyone else.

"Captain Leclere said the same thing to me," said Edmond. "And if you had not asked me, I would not have told you about Elba. Now, sir, may I request a leave of absence? Danglars will see to the listing of cargo."

Morrel smiled. "You wish time off to get married, I believe? I have heard that a lovely young woman named Mercedes waits for you impatiently. Permission granted."

Orders from a Dying Captain

Edmond's delight at this praise of Mercedes' beauty and faithfulness showed in his wide smile. "Yes, sir, we expect to be married at once. But first I must go to Paris to deliver something."

An hour later Edmond was running up the stairs to the tiny apartment he shared with his elderly father. Monsieur Dantes embraced his son and gave thanks for his safe return. Much as the father wanted to hear about the voyage and to enjoy his son's presence, he knew that another shared Edmond's love.

"Go to Mercedes now, my boy," he said. "I will prepare a special dinner for us."

As Edmond hurried to her house, Mercedes was having an unpleasant talk with her cousin Fernand, a soldier. She had endured this same conversation many times since Edmond had sailed. It was Fernand's proposal of marriage. Each time he proposed, she would refuse him and remind him that she loved Edmond. Then

A Son Returns from the Sea.

Fernand would lose his temper, draw his sword, and wave it wildly, swearing to kill Edmond. Sighing at a familiar scene, Mercedes would threaten him again and again that if he hurt Edmond even slightly, her cousinly love for Fernand would change into hatred. Now Mercedes repeated what was always her final statement, "I will never marry anyone but Edmond Dantes."

At this moment Edmond entered and heard her declaration. Mercedes sprang up with a cry of happiness and rushed into Edmond's arms. They kissed and pledged their love anew. Mercedes' eyes shone when Edmond told her he was to be the next captain of the *Pharaon*.

Forgotten in the background, Fernand watched the lovers with bitterness. He hated Edmond Dantes with all his heart, but he could do nothing about it.

Mercedes is True to Edmond.

Fernand Is Full of Hatred.

CHAPTER 2

Arrested!

Finally, unable to bear the sight of the happy couple, Fernand rushed out of the house. Mercedes followed him.

"Dear cousin, I want you to embrace my husband-to-be," she pleaded. "I know he will find a true friend in you, as I did."

Fernand shrank back from this demand. As Edmond came to him with a smile and an outstretched hand, Fernand could only bring himself to touch the hand quickly and coldly. Then he hurried away, hardly watching where he was going. He was so deep in misery that he passed by an inn without noticing Danglars and another man seated at a table outside. Glasses of wine and a half-empty bottle were before them. Danglars called to Fernand and motioned the waiter to bring another glass. At the sound of his name, Fernand looked around wildly as if awakened from a bad dream.

"You called me?" he asked.

The second man at the table was the Dantes' downstairs neighbor, a man named Caderousse. Now he answered Fernand.

"Yes, we called. When we see a young lover running madly through the streets, we know fate has dealt him a blow. So we offer him some wine." With that, Caderousse filled the third glass, but spilled wine as he poured. He had already had seven glasses.

Fernand sat down with a groan. Ignoring the wine, he buried his head in his hands.

"Why didn't the sea swallow him up?" he cried. "Other men leave and never return.

An Invitation to Trouble

Why must Dantes come back to claim Mercedes?"

Caderousse turned to Danglars and winked. "See, Danglars, you have a brother in misery. You are united in your hatred of the handsome and lucky Edmond Dantes."

Danglars had only drunk one glass of wine, so he was still thinking clearly. As he looked at Fernand's agony, his scheming mind began to form a plan for using the unhappy soldier for his own revenge. He said lightly, "In stories, one lover gets rid of a rival by a well-placed knife thrust. But perhaps real men are too timid for that."

Fernand was stung by this insult and looked up angrily. "As a soldier and a man I would not hesitate for one moment to put a knife in Dantes' heart," he cried. "But, alas, Mercedes has forbidden it. I would earn his death and her hatred with the same blow."

"Well, then," said Caderousse cheerfully,

Danglars Schemes for Revenge.

"you will just have to see them married before the *Pharaon* sails again under its new commander, Captain Edmond Dantes!"

This time it was Danglars who looked up angrily. "I will thank you, Caderousse, not to keep mentioning my loss. If certain authorities knew what I know, Dantes would not be made captain. In fact, he would be arrested for conspiring against our good King Louis XVIII."

Danglars saw he had the full attention of the other men, though Caderousse was beginning to succumb to too much wine. Danglars leaned across the table and whispered, "Edmond Dantes stopped the ship at Elba and went ashore to see an enemy of the King, the exiled Napoleon. When he came back on board, he carried a letter. It was no doubt addressed to Napoleon's friends in Paris. Then after we docked, he asked Monsieur Morrel for a leave of absence, not only to get married but to take

A Stop to See Napoleon

something to Paris. It must be that letter."

"Where is the letter now?" asked Fernand, shocked at such dangerous conduct.

"It must be in one of three places," replied Danglars. "Dantes may be carrying it. Or he has left it at his father's apartment. Or it is in his cabin on board ship."

Fernand now went very pale. In a voice shaking with determination he cried, "I shall go the King's Prosecutor here in Marseilles and denounce Edmond Dantes as an enemy of the King!"

Danglars shook his head in disapproval. "They will make you sign your declaration. Then they will put him in prison, but only for a few years. The day that he is freed, he will come looking for you. He will attack you, and you will have to defend yourself. As a soldier, you are experienced in fighting and you may wound him fatally. Mercedes will hate you for that. But then she would already hate you for

"I Shall Denounce Edmond Dantes!"

denouncing him in the first place."

Fernand's shoulders drooped. "You are right. I can do nothing to him."

"There *is* a way to do it, I think," said Danglars. He ordered a waiter to bring pen and ink and paper. Then he wrote a letter with his left hand so his handwriting would not be recognized. He put in all the facts he had told Fernand and Caderousse. He signed the letter "A Friend," folded it in two, and addressed it to the King's Prosecutor.

Fernand took the letter and read it aloud with much satisfaction. Caderousse, though very drunk, made an effort to follow the reading.

"Oh, that is a terrible thing to say," complained Caderousse. "Dantes is my neighbor, and I know this would break his father's heart." He reached out an unsteady hand to grab the letter.

But Danglars quickly snatched it from

An Accusation from "A Friend"

Fernand and crumpled it into a loose ball. Then he said with a laugh, "You are right, friend Caderousse. We were only making a joke. I never meant to send such a document because Dantes is my shipmate." He tossed the crumpled letter into the bushes near the table, then added, "Now I will help you home, for too much wine will cause a man to stagger. Good-bye, Fernand."

Danglars helped Caderousse to his feet and led him away from the inn. The drunken man went willingly but slowly. As they walked up the street, Danglars glanced back. Fernand had risen and was searching in the bushes for the letter. Danglars smiled to himself, well pleased with his own cleverness and judgment of other men.

Near noon the next day, a procession of people in their best clothes walked to that same inn. In the lead was Edmond, his handsome face aglow with happiness. Mercedes

The Letter Is Tossed into the Bushes.

walked at his right, linking her arm with his. She wore a long, flowing white gown. Its style was simple but elegant, making her look more like a Greek goddess than a seventeen-year-old girl of Marseilles. On her head was a circlet of fresh flowers. Her eyes were shining.

Edmond had a single flower pinned to the jacket of his sailor's dress outfit. A similar flower adorned the lapel of old Monsieur Dantes' best black coat. He had brushed the coat well and polished its steel buttons. A three-cornered hat sat on his white hair at a jaunty angle. He walked in the crowd just behind Mercedes.

After them walked Monsieur Morrel, the shipowner, whose presence was a great honor. With him was Fernand, who was so pale that some wondered if he were ill. Then came Caderousse, Danglars, and all the sailors on the *Pharaon*. They were accompanied by their wives and sweethearts. This, then, was the

A Procession to the Inn

procession heading to the engagement luncheon of Edmond and Mercedes.

The inn was closed to outsiders that day, and all the tables had been arranged to form one long one. Mercedes sat midway with Monsieur Dantes and Fernand on either side of her. Edmond sat across from them between Monsieur Morrel and Danglars. The rest of the group seated themselves as they chose, with much noise and good-natured shoving. Toasts to the engaged couple were offered first by Morrel and then by Monsieur Dantes. Soon the innkeeper and his helpers began a parade of special dishes to the celebrators. These dishes included lobster and sausages cooked in five different ways. The platters were decorated with clusters of tomatoes, parsley, and onions.

Edmond and Mercedes were too busy gazing at each other across the table to bother eating. Edmond could not stop smiling, for he

Special Dishes Are Served.

considered himself the happiest man in the world. Caderousse led all the guests in eating heartily... all, that is, except Fernand. He only picked at his food while nervously watching the door that opened to the outside.

After a while, Edmond stood up and took out his pocket watch. "My friends," he announced, "I have a surprise. With Monsieur Morrel's help, Mercedes and I have been able to rush through the many papers required before a marriage may take place. Therefore, this is not an engagement feast you are eating, but a wedding feast." He looked at his watch. "We will be married in exactly one half-hour from now. The mayor awaits us."

This announcement caused a sensation, and several cheers went up. There was one last toast. Then everyone assembled at the door, ready to make the walk to the town hall into a happy parade. One of Edmond's shipmates threw open the door, only to find two soldiers

Edmond's Surprise Announcement

standing there. They pushed the sailor back into the room and motioned the others to move away. A magistrate entered, wearing his official black robe.

"Where is Edmond Dantes?" he asked.

Edmond dropped Mercedes' hand and stepped forward. "Here, sir."

In a cold, official voice the magistrate said, "I arrest you in the name of the law. Follow me." He turned and started out.

Immediately the two soldiers placed themselves one in front and one in back of Edmond and waited for him to obey. Edmond was too shocked to move.

"Arrested? Me? Why, sir?" he cried. "I have done nothing. This must be a mistake."

The magistrate turned back for a moment. "I have been ordered to arrest Edmond Dantes, and I am arresting Edmond Dantes. The reasons will be told to you by the King's Prosecutor. Now, come along."

The Celebration Is Interrupted.

Monsieur Morrel, though greatly disturbed, knew that this was the way the law did things. He whispered, "Go, Edmond. This man is only doing as he has been told. When you see the Prosecutor, it will all be cleared up."

These words calmed Edmond, and he said almost cheerfully to the magistrate, "Sir, I am at your service. I wish that we might go quickly so that I may return the sooner. I have important business to attend to in a half hour."

At this, there were laughter and cheers. Several sailors shook Edmond's hand, and the women waved their handkerchiefs. But Mercedes had turned pale. Edmond gave her a quick smile and with head held high, he marched out between the soldiers.

Edmond Is Arrested.

Monsieur Dantes Collapses.

CHAPTER 3

The Assistant Prosecutor

As Edmond departed, old Monsieur Dantes collapsed in a half-faint. He had been in poor health, and the excitement of having Edmond home and about to be married had overtired him. Now the horror of seeing his beloved son marched away between soldiers proved too much.

A chair was brought, and the old man was helped into it. Mercedes rubbed his hands to warm them.

"Dear Father, calm yourself," she said. "Edmond will return in a short while. You saw how he smiled. It is some silly mistake. Perhaps the person responsible for it is apologizing at this moment."

Monsieur Dantes looked into her eyes. He saw the same fear in them that he knew showed in his own. "No, Mercedes," he whispered, "I feel something terrible is going to happen to Edmond."

Hearing the old man speak her own fears, Mercedes turned from him and buried her face in her hands. A sob escaped her.

Seeing the terrified old man and young girl, Caderousse frowned. He tried to remember exactly what had happened at the table outside the inn the day before. It was hard because he had been in a drunken haze. But enough realization of what was going on had come through. He whispered to Danglars, "This is some part of the trick you were going to play, you and Fernand. It is shameful!"

Danglars looked at him coldly. "I know

Caderousse Suspects Danglars' Trick.

nothing about this arrest. Your drinking has confused you. Be quiet!"

Since Monsieur Morrel was an important person, he knew that he might be able to find out the reason for Edmond's arrest. So he had followed the soldiers and their prisoner. Now as he returned to the inn, a worried expression clouded his face. He went straight to Monsieur Dantes and Mercedes. "My friends," he said solemnly, "a very serious charge has been made against Edmond. Someone has accused him of being a secret agent for Napoleon and thus a traitor to the King!"

Meanwhile, in the office of the Assistant Prosecutor, these same accusing words were being said to Edmond Dantes. The Prosecutor himself was ill in bed and had sent his capable assistant, Monsieur Villefort, to deal with the matter. The two men were alone in the room, though soldiers stood on guard outside the door.

Monsieur Morrel Brings Bad News.

Edmond stared in amazement at the Assistant Prosecutor. "No, sir, I am not a secret agent. I have no political opinions. I am only a sailor, and my concerns are my ship, my father, and my intended wife."

Villefort, older than Edmond by only ten years, was impressed by the sincere way in which Edmond uttered his statement. Villefort also saw intelligence in Edmond's face, though he realized the young man's education was confined to matters of the sea and sailing. Finally, it was of interest to him that he and Edmond shared a coincidence. Both had been celebrating their wedding feasts and had been interrupted in the middle of the festivities. Villefort's mind wandered for a moment to the lovely, rich young noblewoman he was to marry.

Then Villefort brought his thoughts back to his duty. "Tell me, Monsieur Dantes, why did you stop the *Pharaon* at Elba and pick up a

"I Am Not a Secret Agent."

letter there?"

Edmond told his story so convincingly that Villefort believed him. He asked to see the letter, but Edmond hesitated.

"I have sworn, sir, to give this letter only to the person to whom it is addressed," he explained. "It is a man in Paris."

Edmond's loyalty increased Villefort's admiration for him. It was obvious that the young sailor was a person of honor and that his claim to innocence was completely true. Villefort smiled reassuringly. "I represent the law here, and the law commands you to hand over the letter. In doing so, you will not break your word because my soldiers could take it from you by force. Give me the letter with your conscience clear."

At these words Edmond smiled too. "I give you the letter gladly, sir. Though you are the law, you respect a man's honor." From the inside pocket of his jacket Edmond brought

Edmond Hands Over the Letter.

out a sealed white envelope and handed it to Villefort.

The Assistant Prosecutor turned away from Edmond toward the lamp on his desk so he would have more light by which to read the name on the envelope. Thus Edmond did not see the look of horror which came over Villefort's face when he read the name. Fearing for a moment that he might faint, Villefort steadied himself against his desk. He dared to read the name again and the familiar address in Paris. It still read "TO MONSIEUR NOIRTIER." The letter was addressed to Villefort's *father*!

Villefort had often told himself that one day this moment would happen—the moment when all he had worked for would vanish and he would be disgraced. But lately, as he became rich and attained the position of Assistant Prosecutor, he thought less and less about that moment. The final step into a

A Shocking Name!

secure life was his engagement to Renee.

He had used his mother's name, Villefort, on coming to Marseilles, so no one connected him with the notorious traitor, Noirtier, who was loyal to Napoleon. Politically, Noirtier had been quiet for years, but as Villefort now read in the letter, his father was to come out of hiding and lead a plot to restore Napoleon to the throne.

As a loyal subject of the King, Villefort could not allow the letter to be delivered, but neither could he bring himself to have his own father arrested. This was not because he loved him, but because he feared that the connection between them would inevitably be revealed. Villefort made his decision quickly, then turned back to Edmond.

"Who has seen this letter beside yourself?" he asked in a calm voice.

Edmond answered with surprise, "I told you, sir. No one has seen it. I myself have not

"No One Has Seen the Letter."

read the letter since it was sealed. But no one has even seen the envelope since I received it."

Inwardly Villefort gave thanks. He also gave thanks for the illness of his superior—an illness which had prevented the Prosecutor from coming to the office today. If *he* had read the letter, Villefort would have been a ruined man. But now, Villefort began to hope. He smiled at Edmond again and lowered his voice.

"I believe you, Dantes. But having this letter as evidence is awkward. It is the only thing that supports the accusation made against you in this note we received." He handed Edmond the note written by Danglars with his left hand. Though the note was crumpled, Fernand had smoothed it out before he sent it. The signature still read "A Friend," with no further identification.

Edmond read it and shook his head in bewilderment. "I don't know who could have written this," he said.

Edmond Reads the Accusation.

Villefort returned the accusation to a folder marked "Edmond Dantes." Then he took up the letter addressed to his father and turned it over in his hands, as if trying to decide a deep problem. Suddenly he winked at Edmond and strode to the fireplace. He tossed the letter into the flames. "I believed you are innocent, Dantes. Therefore I destroy the only evidence that exists against you." As Villefort saw the name "Noirtier" disappear into ashes, his heart beat normally again.

"Thank you, sir," said Edmond. "You are more like my true friend than the King's Prosecutor."

"But now," said Villefort, returning to his desk, "you must take my advice. You must swear never to mention this letter or the name to whom it was addressed. Only you and I know it once existed."

"I swear to tell no one," agreed Edmond eagerly. "If anyone questions me, I will deny

Villefort Burns the Evidence.

such a letter ever existed."

"Now I must detain you a short while longer until I have written a report," said Villefort, as an afterthought. He rang for the captain of the guards, then said something to him in a low tone of voice so Edmond could not hear. To Edmond he said, "Go with him, Dantes."

Edmond saluted Villefort and followed the captain of the guards with a light heart. He counted himself a lucky man to have had his case heard by the Assistant Prosecutor rather than the Prosecutor. Villefort had said he must only stay "a short while longer." Perhaps in an hour or less he would be back at Mercedes' side.

Whispered Instructions

A Prisoner in a Cell

CHAPTER 4

The Chateau d'If

The captain led Edmond across a court-yard and into an unheated building. Its windows were small and barred. As the captain passed, soldiers stood at attention. After walking down two flights of stairs, Edmond was motioned into a bare room, with a table and a cot as its only furnishings. After the captain shut the door, Edmond heard a bolt being drawn. He was a prisoner in a cell. But Edmond was not worried by his situation, for the Assistant Prosecutor himself had declared him innocent. Edmond sat down on the cot to wait.

As the hours passed, Edmond consulted his watch more and more anxiously. He was especially concerned that his father and Mercedes would be worrying about him. He kept reminding himself of the kindness and understanding that Villefort had shown.

Finally, six hours later, the bolt was drawn. Four armed soldiers summoned him out. Edmond stepped eagerly into the corridor, but was not led back to Villefort's office as he expected. Instead, he was led upstairs and into the dark street where a carriage waited. Certain that there must be another mistake, Edmond hesitated to climb in. But the soldiers gave him a shove, and he climbed in quickly. Two soldiers placed themselves on either side of him, and the carriage set off.

Soon Edmond began to smell the sea, and he knew they were nearing the docks. In another moment the carriage stopped. Edmond was

Forced into a Carriage

hustled out and pushed toward a waiting rowboat, manned by four men. A soldier waiting on the dock appeared to be in charge. He listened to the instructions whispered by the two soldiers and nodded.

"Where are you taking me?" asked Edmond, now very alarmed. He was sure he had been mistaken for another prisoner. "I am Edmond Dantes."

"We know," said the man in charge of the boat. "Get in." He put a hand on Edmond's shoulder and forced him to jump down into the boat. He followed Edmond in, then gave the command to shove off.

The only point of light Edmond could see on the water was the lighthouse. But the rowers did not strain their eyes to see in the dark. They pulled steadily and confidently as if the course they rowed was a familiar one.

After his long confinement in the small cell, Edmond was grateful to smell the fresh sea

Pushed into a Rowboat

air. But why should he be in a rowboat in the middle of the night, going he did not know where?

"Where are you taking me?" he demanded angrily. "Does Monsieur Villefort know what you are doing?"

These questions annoyed the man in charge, for he frowned. "Don't pretend," he answered. "You come from Marseilles, don't you? Everybody knows that pile of rocks." He gestured toward a dark fortress that they were approaching. It was the only structure on the small, rocky island just outside the harbor.

Edmond looked where he pointed, then turned back with a gasp. "Not the Chateau d'If! Why that is *a prison*!"

At this last statement the man laughed. "And you, my friend, are a *prisoner*."

"But I am innocent of any crime," protested Edmond wildly. "I have not even had a trial! Monsieur Villefort released me!"

The Chateau d'If — a Prison!

The boat scraped against stone steps. One sailor jumped out and tied the boat to a ring cemented to a massive stone wall. With a nod, the man in charge indicated that Edmond was to proceed up the steps. He did so in a daze. At the top of the steps the man in charge kicked at a heavy door. After a wait of some minutes, the door swung open to receive their party. Another door, guarded by two soldiers, barred their way. After a whispered consultation with the boatman, one soldier took Edmond by the elbow and led him through the second doorway.

Thus, on the 28th of February, 1815, Edmond Dantes entered the Chateau d'If.

Arriving at the Chateau d'If

Edmond Is Bewildered.

CHAPTER 5

Number 34

Edmond was hurried down steep stone steps into a cell. Dampness and evil odors surrounded him. By the light of the jailor's lantern he saw that the cell contained a chair, a table, a pail, and a cot with straw and a blanket thrown on top. While one jailor brought in some bread and a jug of water, another stood guard. But it was not necessary, for Edmond was so bewildered by what was happening to him that he was too weak to move and too dazed to even breathe. When the jailors left and he heard the iron door clang shut, he sank to the floor where he had been standing.

The next morning, Edmond's jailor found him still hunched over on the stone floor. He had not eaten or drunk or slept. When the jailor poked him, the spell of confusion broke at last, and Edmond wept wildly.

When the jailor had gone, Edmond screamed at his closed door, demanding to know what crime he had committed. After a time, he sank into a despairing heap and stared at the floor again.

When his jailor returned and saw that he had not eaten, he spoke encouragingly to him. The jailor was paid according to the number of prisoners he had to care for. If Edmond should die of starvation, the jailor's salary would be reduced. "You must keep up your strength," he told Edmond. "Perhaps in a year or two they will let you appeal your sentence. Others have been permitted to do so."

Screaming at a Closed Door

"A year or two!" Edmond was shocked. "I must speak to Monsieur Villefort *now*. Listen, please. I will pay you to take a message to him. And another one to a young girl called Mercedes in Marseilles."

The jailor laughed loudly. "I would be fired if I were caught carrying messages for prisoners," he explained. "You could not pay me enough to make me endanger my job. There is one prisoner here, a mad priest, who frequently offers me a million francs to help him."

Now Edmond stood up, showing himself to be a strong young man. He said in a quiet but positive manner, "If you do not help me, one time when you enter this cell, I will be behind the door. I will seize you and choke the life out of you."

At this, the jailor ran from the cell. He returned a few minutes later with six soldiers, all armed with guns. The soldiers forced

No Messages Are Carried Out.

Edmond from the cell and thrust him into a dungeon at the end of a dark corridor. There, Edmond closed his eyes and wondered if he were going mad.

The days and nights passed slowly for Edmond. His jailors hardly spoke to him, and they never used his name. He was known simply as "Number 34," for that was the number of his dungeon. Starved for conversation, Edmond begged his jailor for a few words. But the man merely shook his head "no," put down the day's meal, and did not even glance at Edmond. Edmond talked out loud to himself constantly. Once, he had pitied galley-slaves, but now he saw that they had some happiness. At least they breathed the sea air, and they had one another for companionship. Edmond had nothing.

A year passed this way, and Edmond stopped trying to keep track of the date. He begged his jailors to let him go for a walk, to

Prisoner Number 34

give him books, anything to pass the time. But his pleas were refused. Then he began to think about religion and pleaded with his jailor to permit him to see the prisoner they called "the mad priest." He is still a man of the church, thought Edmond, and he will guide me in my prayers for release. But this visit was never permitted.

Another year passed, and Edmond grew furious with his lot in life. He stopped praying and began to curse everyone who might have acted to imprison him. But he was so uneducated and so inexperienced in wordly matters that he could not imagine who would have wanted to harm him. Being young, he did not have many memories, so his boredom with his own thoughts became more intense.

As the years passed, four...six...eight ...ten, Edmond feared he was going mad. Sometime in his twelfth year, Edmond came to a decision. "I wish to die," he said aloud. "I

Praying for Freedom

swear that I shall never eat or drink again."
When his dinner was brought that evening,
Edmond threw it out the small, barred window into the sea. He was intent on keeping his
jailor from knowing what was happening, for
he feared the prison authorities might order
him fed by force. For a whole week he threw
out his food and drink, but the lack of water
quickly sickened him. As Edmond grew weaker and weaker, it was all he could do to totter
to the window and empty out his dish and
mug. His jailor saw his weakness and thought
he must be wasting away from some terrible
illness.

Finally one evening Edmond felt sure his
end was near. He was almost happy as he
drifted into a kind of twilight of half-sleeping
and half-waking. Silently he blessed his father
and Mercedes. His breathing grew more and
more shallow. In another hour, the suffering
and the life of Number 34 would be over.

"I Shall Never Eat or Drink Again."

Hearing Scraping Behind the Wall

CHAPTER 6

Scrape...Scrape...Scrape

As Edmond lay dying on his cot, he heard a noise—a constant scraping. His dungeon was infested with rats and large bugs, but this scraping was different from any of their sounds. Edmond raised his head weakly and listened harder. The sound was like a large claw scraping on the stone wall near his cot.

His heart gave a great lurch as he realized that some prisoner was attempting to escape! The thought of someone making his way to freedom made Edmond feel dizzy. He told himself that his weakness was making him hear things. But the sound continued. It cannot be a workman for the prison, Edmond reasoned, because it is the middle of the night.

His starving body then caused him to fall into a disturbed sleep.

He awoke in the morning angry with himself. Perhaps some fellow sufferer was trying to signal him and he had not heard. When the jailor brought his breakfast, Edmond gobbled it up. His desire for death had vanished. Now his one thought was to make contact with whoever was scraping.

After breakfast, Edmond waited tensely by the wall for an hour. Then it came! Scrape . . . scrape . . . scrape. . . . He leaped up and grabbed his chair. Knocking the back of the chair against the wall, he made a clunking noise. He did it three times. At once the scraping stopped. Edmond knocked three times more. Trembling, he waited to hear something, anything. For an hour he stood

A Knock to Answer a Scrape

there holding the chair, ready to respond.

At last the sound behind the wall came again. In a fever of joy Edmond beat the back of the chair against the wall. Then he stopped suddenly, fearful that a jailor might hear him. To calm his rapidly beating heart, he threw himself down on his cot. There, he reproached himself for wasting twelve years by never trying to escape as the man behind his wall was trying.

This thought propelled Edmond off his cot and into a search for something to scrape with. His cot had iron clamps, but they were screwed tightly into the wood. His eyes lit up when he saw his water mug. Without hesitation, he dropped the mug onto the stone floor. It broke, and Edmond selected the largest and sharpest fragment. Then he attacked the wall with it. The scraping on the other side was so much like a companionship that Edmond found himself crying

A Broken Mug for a Scraping Tool

with happiness.

The plaster that held the stones of the wall together was crumbly from age and from the dampness of the dungeon. Edmond scraped vigorously and was soon rewarded by a shower of plaster dust and small pieces of stone. He worked through the day. Before his jailor arrived with dinner, he moved his bed to conceal the loosening stone. He trickled the plaster dust out the window, then hid his scraper under his blanket and lay down on top of it.

Edmond was given another mug. The jailor did not notice that one large piece of the broken mug was missing when he swept the fragments from the dungeon. After dinner Edmond waited an hour before daring to go back to his task. While he waited, he rested because he was still weak from starving himself.

This pattern continued for the next two days. By then, Edmond had cleared all the

Chipping Away at the Plaster

plaster from the sides of one stone. But when he tried to move the huge slab, his fingers could not budge it. He needed a lever to work the stone out. Desperately Edmond examined his dungeon. Nothing! "I cannot fail now," he told himself, pacing back and forth in his anxiety.

The jailors had begun bringing around dinner. The clank of their utensils came to Edmond's ears along with an idea. His nightly soup was brought in an iron pot. Its iron handle would make a perfect lever. But the jailor usually poured his soup from this pot into his plate and took the pot away with him.

"Suppose," Edmond whispered to himself with a wild surge of hope, "just suppose I did not have a plate." Quickly he put his plate in front of the door, then flung himself on his cot to watch and hope.

Edmond's jailor entered. All his attention was centered on not spilling the soup, so he did

The Huge Stone Won't Budge.

not see the plate before his heavy foot crunched down on it.

"Look what you have made me do," complained the jailor. "You have left your plate in my way. First your mug, now your plate. Do you think our citizens have nothing to do with their tax money but buy you dishes?" He was angry with Edmond but also with himself, for it was his foot that broke the dish. "All right, take the pot for your soup plate. See if you can keep *that* in one piece."

Edmond almost fainted with joy. At most, he had hoped to have the iron pot for one night. Now it was to be his permanently. That night, he levered the big stone out easily with the pot handle and set to work scraping around the next stone. A passageway began to form with the first stone being moved in and out to conceal the entrance. Edmond found that the stones beyond it could be pushed under a wooden beam that arched in

The Jailor Brings a Soup Pot.

back of the wall.

The day came when Edmond and the first scraper were working on the same stone from opposite ends. Edmond scraped with almost insane energy until they moved the last stone aside.

On their knees in the passageway, the two prisoners faced one another. They stretched out trembling hands and touched. Edmond drew the other man forward while he inched backward toward his entrance. Back in his dungeon, Edmond reached down and helped the other man to his feet.

"Who are you?" Edmond asked. His voice shook so, that he had to repeat the question.

The man answered, "I am Father Faria. The jailors call me 'The Mad Priest.' "

Trembling Hands Touch.

Father Faria, "The Mad Priest"

CHAPTER 7

The Mad Priest

"The Mad Priest" was rather short. His hair was white from suffering, but his beard, which reached down to his chest, was still black. Yet he was probably sixty-five years old. His eyes burned, not with madness as the jailors said, but with intelligence. At once Edmond poured out the story of his imprisonment. Then it was Father Faria's turn.

The priest had been at the Chateau d'If sixteen years, four years longer than Edmond. He was Italian, a man of the church, and learned. Political enemies had caused his arrest after the death of the rich Cardinal Spada, who had protected Faria and treated him like a son.

As he listened, Edmond felt that his whole world had turned over, now that he had a friend. He dared to say "friend" even though Faria was so much older and so much better educated than he. Edmond would never have dared consider such a man his friend back in Marseilles. On his side, Faria was warmed by Edmond's youth and admiration for him.

For the next few weeks the two men used the passageway freely to go between Edmond's dungeon and the priest's cell. This cell was a larger and fitter place to live than the dungeon, since Faria was not considered dangerous, only mad, by his jailors.

Edmond was in a constant state of amazement at the priest's accomplishments. Faria had made a rope ladder, using the threads unraveled from his blanket. The sharp bone of

Becoming Friends

a fish had been fashioned into a needle. Cartilage, or tissue fibers, from other fish were made into pens, and an unused fireplace provided soot for ink. With such writing tools Faria had covered all of his shirts and handkerchiefs with his political ideas on the government in Italy. Sometimes he even used his own blood to write with. Finally, he showed Edmond his main accomplishment—a razor-sharp knife made from a candlestick.

As all these treasures were laid before Edmond, he began to weep at his own inferiority. Not only was he ignorant of everything written on Faria's cloth, but also he had wasted his prison years in idleness.

At Edmond's confession Faria's eyes shone, for he loved to teach. At once he formed a plan for Edmond's education. He, himself, knew four languages and had read widely in all of them. He was determined to pass them and all that he knew of mathematics, physics, and

Father Faria's Accomplishments

history on to Edmond.

During the next year and a half, Faria taught, and Edmond made rapid progress. He was delighted to find within himself a love of learning, and he worked hard at his studies. Another change occurred in him. Without realizing it, he began to adopt Faria's refined quiet way of speaking and moving. Soon the rough sailor vanished, and an educated young gentleman emerged.

With his newly found powers of thinking Edmond also plotted their escape. They would tunnel into the corridor in front of Faria's cell. In the middle of the night they would burst out of the tunnel and overpower the two guards who always sat half-asleep at a table. Dressed in the guards' uniforms and using their keys, they would make their way out of the prison. Then they would jump into the sea and swim to safety. The two friends shook hands on it.

Edmond's Education

"I Have Been Thinking About My Enemies."

The Treasure on Monte Cristo

Weeks . . . then months went by. One day as Edmond and Faria rested from the hard work of tunneling, Edmond said, "Father, I have been thinking about my enemies. Your lessons on history have taught me how the minds of some men work in evil ways. I believe I was accused by two men—Danglars and Fernand. Danglars saw me carry the letter away from Elba, and he had hoped to be captain of the *Pharaon* until I was chosen. Fernand hated me because Mercedes had consented to be my wife and not his. I could confirm these suspicions if I could talk to our old neighbor, Caderousse. I saw him after my return, sitting and drinking with Danglars and Fernand. They may have been talking about me, for as I passed the inn, they stopped talking and pretended not to notice me."

"Very good thinking," said Faria with a smile. "When you told me everything about yourself, I, too, suspected Danglars and Fernand. But I wanted you to puzzle it out."

Edmond went on. "There is one part of the puzzle I have not figured out. Why did Monsieur Villefort shut me up here forever when he appeared to believe my story and agreed I was innocent?"

Faria nodded thoughtfully. "True. There is also something curious about his burning the letter from Elba. Why should the Assistant Prosecutor for the King destroy evidence as a favor to a sailor he had never met before?"

"He must have feared me for some reason,"

"They Pretended Not to Notice Me."

answered Edmond. "But that is ridiculous. How could I harm such an important man?"

Faria was silent for a moment. "You knew only one secret—the name of the traitor to whom the letter was addressed."

"Yes, Father, but the name was that of a stranger, Noirtier."

At this, Father Faria groaned and lifted his arms to Heaven. "There it is!" he cried. "There is the reason! I know this traitor Noirtier. He is the father of Villefort, who is so ashamed of the old man that he uses his mother's family name."

At this revelation of the reason for Villefort's betrayal of him, Edmond became very pale. He leaned toward Faria and said urgently, "I must have revenge! I must destroy these three men who have taken away my youth and given me fourteen years of suffering in return. Let us double our working time on the tunnel."

"I Know This Traitor Noirtier!"

From then on, the work on the tunnel went rapidly. When they reached the last stone, which would give them access to the corridor, they scraped only a certain amount of plaster. They would remove the rest on the night of the escape. Until then, the stone had to remain fixed in its usual place.

As they rejoiced at coming to the end of the tunneling, Faria staggered. Edmond dragged the half-fainting priest back to his cell and put him on his cot. Faria seemed not to be breathing. Hearing the jailors approach, Edmond lowered himself back into the tunnel, and, just before pulling the entrance stone into place, he called loudly, "Help! I am ill."

For the next few days Edmond dared not use the tunnel. He was torn with anxiety about Father Faria. Was he alive or dead? Edmond kept his ear to the door of his dungeon as much as possible. Finally he was rewarded by overhearing two jailors as they

A Sudden Illness

talked.

"I like him, though he is mad," said one.

"Yes, it is too bad to see him paralyzed like that," said the other.

Edmond's heart sank when he heard this news, but then it lifted, because Faria was still alive.

A month went by before Edmond heard the old scraping behind his wall. Quickly he moved the entrance stone and admitted the priest into his dungeon. They wept and embraced each other. Then Edmond wept some more when he saw that Faria's right arm and leg were paralyzed.

But Faria calmed him. The old man had dragged himself with the greatest of difficulty to Edmond for one reason—to urge Edmond to escape alone that very night.

Edmond drew himself up, his eyes flashing. "My only friend, I swear never to leave you. While I waited for this reunion, I made a plan.

Faria Urges Edmond to Escape Alone.

We will fashion some kind of raft from our blankets and fish bones. We will escape as planned, and I will tow you through the water on the raft."

Faria's eyes filled with tears again. "You are my true son. But I will be too great a burden. Go now, alone."

Edmond was firm in his refusal. He helped Faria back to his cell and promised to come later that night to begin the raft.

When Edmond appeared, Faria was studying a drawing on a piece of cloth. The priest beckoned to Edmond and put his hand on the young man's head, as if in a blessing. Very solemnly he announced, "Edmond Dantes, sailor of Marseilles and my adopted son, I declare you my heir. At my death, all the riches that I inherited from Cardinal Spada will belong to you. I do this in gratitude for your love and loyalty."

He then explained the drawing, which was

Faria Declares Edmond His Heir.

a treasure map. It showed one cave among many, and in that cave, one stone among many. When pushed aside, the stone would reveal a corridor. Four feet farther on, a concealed spring would open an entranceway into the room where the Spada treasure lay. When the priest was sure that Edmond had memorized the map, he burned it to ashes.

Edmond had listened obediently but with fear in his heart. Surely this was the talk of a madman! When Faria told him the amount of money that the jewels, gold bars, and silver household objects would bring, Edmond was certain the jailors had been right.

"Seventy million francs?" he repeated. "It cannot be. Father, you must rest."

Faria knew what Edmond was thinkng and waved his hand impatiently. "My son, I am not mad. I know I will never leave the Chateau d'If alive. So let me finish the information. The cave is located on the Island of Monte Cristo.

The Map of Monte Cristo

Do you know it?"

"Yes," said Edmond. "The *Pharaon* passed it often. It is small and uninhabited."

Faria nodded and asked Edmond to help him to his cot. As he lay down, his pale face twisted with pain. With his last breath he gasped, "Farewell, my son. Do not forget Monte Cristo."

Edmond stood frozen at his friend's bedside until dawn when the sounds of stirring by the jailors sent him flying back into the passageway. There, he heard the jailor order Faria's body to be sewn inside a shroud and buried that very evening.

Once back in his own cell, Edmond gave way to his grief. Alone! He was alone once more! So, for the second time in his life Edmond Dantes resolved to die rather than continue to live in misery.

Having been forced to leave Faria's cell so rapidly, Edmond had not had time to say a

"Farewell, My Son."

proper farewell to his dear friend. The soldiers had left, and he determined to see the beloved face once more by chancing one more trip through the passageway. It did not matter if he were caught. His life was over too. So Edmond returned to Faria's cell.

"If only I could die too!" he cried upon seeing the priest completely encased in a thick woolen shroud. "Then I would leave this dungeon just as you are about to do, my dear friend."

As he uttered these words, Edmond was struck by a sudden and terrifying idea. "My God," he murmured. "I must *not* die now. I must punish my executioners first. Since it is only the dead who go free from here, I must take the place of the dead!"

"I Must Take the Place of the Dead!"

A Farewell Kiss

CHAPTER 9

The Cemetery of the Chateau d'If

Edmond carefully undid the stitches that enclosed the shroud and kissed Faria's forehead. Then he ripped open the shroud down its entire length. Gently lifting the corpse, he half-pulled, half-carried it through the tunnel into his dungeon.

He arranged the corpse on his cot and covered it with his blanket so Faria's gray hair did not show. He often lay thus, not turning when his jailor brought dinner in. The man had always ignored him, satisfied to see that his prisoner was still there.

Panting from tension and from his exertion, Edmond rushed back to Faria's cell. The dinner hour was nearing, and the jailors would soon come by. He grabbed Faria's knife, needle, and thread from their hiding place under a stone and jumped into the shroud. Pulling its sides together around him, he began stitching from his feet up. He worked feverishly because he could hear the jailors coming closer, delivering dinners.

Edmond sewed faster and faster. He had put in the last stitch over his head and clapped his hands to his sides just as the jailors reached Faria's cell. As they passed, they were silent out of respect for the dead. Edmond was sure they would hear his heart beating.

But they passed on. Edmond's hand closed on the knife handle. He assumed that the men who would be burying him would not over-work themselves by digging very far down into the rocky soil. The soil they piled on him would

Stitching Himself into the Shroud

be airy enough for him to breathe until they left. Then his knife would easily cut him free from the grave. If, however, on the way to the cemetery, the carriers became aware they held a live body, he was determined to rip open the sack and attack them with his knife.

Dinner time passed, and Edmond's heart slowed a bit. No alarm had been sounded, so when the jailor had brought dinner to Number 34, he must have believed the body on the cot to be a sleeping Edmond.

Somewhere near midnight, Edmond heard the door open. Men with lanterns entered Faria's cell. Edmond held his breath. He felt someone grab him under the shoulders and another take his feet. They swung him onto a stretcher placed on the floor.

One of the men gave a grunt. "He's heavy for an old man. It's good we don't have far to go."

Edmond felt the stretcher being lifted. He

"He's Heavy for an Old Man."

was carried from the cell, down the corridor around corners, and up some stairs. He heard two large doors open before him and bang shut after him. Cold air penetrated the woolen shroud, and he heard the waves breaking on rocks. After fourteen years, he was out of the Chateau d'If.

The stretcher swayed and dipped as the two carriers stumbled on the rocky ground. They stopped. One man held Edmond's feet in the air while the other tied a rope around his ankles. A heavy weight of some kind was put in the stretcher next to his feet, and the rope was knotted to it. The men picked up the stretcher again, breathing more heavily because of the added weight and because they were walking up an incline. The sound of the waves became louder.

"Let's do it from here," said one.

"No," said the other. "Up a bit higher. They made such a fuss about that last one we let fall

Attaching a Heavy Weight to the Body

on the rocks that we better get the Mad Priest far out to sea."

At these words Edmond's heart started pounding even faster. He was not to be buried in the earth, but in *water*. The sea was the cemetery of the Chateau d'If!

They put down the stretcher. Edmond was gripped under the shoulders and by the feet. He was swung to and fro, to and fro.

"One, two, three, and away!" the men chanted together and let go of Edmond.

He flew through the air. Out . . . out . . . and then down. Edmond screamed in terror, a scream that was soon swallowed up in the roar of the waves. The iron weight tied to his ankles pulled him feet-first into the ice-cold water. Edmond held his breath.

Even before his whole body entered the water, Edmond had begun ripping open the shroud. But he could not free himself because of the weight tied to it. He was dragged deep-

The Cemetery of the Chateau d'If

er and deeper under the waves. With tremendous effort Edmond bent and sliced the rope between his ankles. He was suffocating. In another second his mouth would open, and the sea would pour into him. Suddenly the weight dropped off, and his body shot to the surface.

Edmond drank in great gulps of air, all the while moving his feet vigorously to keep himself afloat. He didn't dare stay above water for more than a few seconds at a time. He dove beneath the waves and swam harder and faster than ever before in his life. Forced to surface for air, he looked back at the cliff from which he had been thrown. He could barely make out two figures against lantern light. Edmond doubted that they could spot him in the dark, but he swam underwater again as a safety measure.

The next time he surfaced, he was a good distance from the Chateau d'If. It had started

Slicing the Weight from His Ankles

to rain, and a rumble of thunder came from the left. Edmond remembered another rocky island outside the harbor—a twin of the prison island, but uninhabited—and he headed for it at a steady pace. He wanted shelter from the approaching storm, and he also feared a cramp from the cold water. The thought that he might drown now that he was free gave Edmond strength.

The storm broke just as his feet touched the rocky bottom of the shallow water. Torrents of rain engulfed him as he staggered onto the beach and sank down. Though he was near exhaustion, he quickly crept toward a rock overhang where he would be protected from the lightning that was flashing across the sky. He fell asleep instantly.

In an hour, an especially loud clap of thunder woke Edmond. He shivered in his wet clothes, and he was hungry and thirsty. Lifting his face to the rain, he was able to take in

Swimming for His Life

some water. Then he slept again.

When Edmond awoke the second time, the storm was over. His fears returned with a jolt because now it was daylight. His jailors would have discovered his untouched dinner and Faria's corpse. A search must be underway at this moment.

In the bright morning light the Chateau d'If stood out black and forbidding. As Edmond stared at it, he imagined the activity within. The jailors would probably search the island he was on, first examining the smaller rocks that peppered the sea between it and the prison's island. Then they would go on to Marseilles as the next logical place.

Edmond began to despair. He had lost his knife, his clothes were in rags, and he felt weak from lack of food. Even if he could reach Marseilles, did he dare show himself there? Edmond scrambled from rock to rock, trying to shield himself as much as possible in case

The Jailors Discover Edmond's Escape.

someone with a spyglass should happen to notice movement on an island known to be uninhabited. He found parts of a wrecked ship, a beam with the ship's name, a red woolen sailor's cap, and nothing else.

Suddenly Edmond gasped. A small white cloud rose from the Chateau d'If. It was followed a few seconds later by the burst of a gun. It was the alarm for him!

Just then, another movement caught his eye. A large, fast sailboat of the type used by smugglers was leaving the harbor of the island he was on. Edmond had to make an instant decision. The smugglers might turn him in for the reward, but at least it was a chance for escape!

He jammed the red cap on his head and picked up the large wooden beam bearing the ship's name. Ignoring the cuts of sharp-edged rocks, he ran back into the sea. Holding the beam, he swam toward the boat.

The Alarm Gun Sounds.

A Call for Help

CHAPTER 10

On Monte Cristo At Last!

Edmond swam on a course that would intercept the boat. As he neared it, he flung himself half out of the water and yelled. His calls were heard, and the boat turned to steer in his direction. But in raising himself out of the water to hail the boat, Edmond had expended his last bit of strength.

Just as a rowboat was being lowered for him, Edmond lost his grasp on the beam which had helped him stay afloat, and he began to sink.

"Help! Help!" he called, struggling to the

surface.

The rowers doubled their efforts.

As Edmond was about to sink again, the rowboat reached him. One rower called to him in Italian, "Courage!" Edmond was too weak to lift a hand for the men to grab, so the Italian who had spoken to him seized his long hair and kept his face above water. In another moment the others had hauled Edmond into the boat where he immediately lost consciousness.

Edmond did not waken until he was aboard the large sailboat. The Italian sailor, Jacopo, was pouring rum down his throat. Edmond sputtered and came to his senses. As he gasped his thanks to his rescuers, he saw that they were, as he had feared, smugglers. The captain was suspicious and looked back and forth from Edmond to the puffs of smoke of the alarm gun at the Chateau d'If.

Edmond had to come up with a story

Edmond Comes to His Senses.

quickly. "I am from Malta," he gasped, "and I was shipwrecked in the storm last night. My captain and shipmates were all drowned, but I was able to cling to a piece of wood from our ship. You can still see it floating out there."

Jacopo interrupted. "I almost didn't grab you. With that long hair and beard you looked frightening."

Edmond silently blessed Father Faria for having sharpened his wits, because he could now come up with a logical answer at a moment's notice. He explained, "Once, in a moment of danger, I made a vow not to cut my hair or beard for ten years if I was saved. And I was. That ten years is up today, and thanks to you, I am rescued and can now cut both."

The captain was still thoughtful. "What am I to do with you?" he said.

"I am a sailor. Maybe you can use someone who has sailed these waters for years."

The captain's eyes gleamed. "Can you set a

Explaining His Hair and Beard

course? And do you know the best harbors?"

Edmond nodded. "Certainly. I will prove my worth to you right now. Why do you zigzag your ship so much? It wastes time."

"If I didn't," answered the captain with a superior smile, "we would run straight into the Island of Rion."

Edmond stood up. "Let me take the wheel. I will steer a straight and fast course, and we will *not* hit Rion."

The captain's attention had now shifted completely away from the alarm gun. "All right, show me what kind of sailor you are."

Edmond took the wheel and gave orders about the amount of sail. Gaining speed, he steered the ship past Rion, coming close but not dangerously so.

"Well done," said the captain, very impressed. Jacopo and some others gave a cheer, for they enjoyed good seamanship.

After this proof of his abilities, Edmond was

Edmond Steers a Straight, Fast Course.

hired for the duration of the voyage to Leghorn, a city on the western coast of Italy. Jacopo gave him trousers and a shirt. The Italian sailor had adopted Edmond as a special friend since it was he who had rescued him.

By the time the ship reached Leghorn, Edmond was rejoicing again in the life of a free sailor. The captain entrusted the ship more and more to him, for everyone could see that Edmond's seamanship was superior.

At Leghorn, the captain begged Edmond to stay with him, and he did so. They took on cotton and tobacco, on which no duty had been paid, and sailed with that cargo to the island of Corsica. There, they smuggled it to another ship, which planned to carry it to France. For this venture, all hands received one hundred francs apiece and were highly pleased.

Edmond made several other voyages with illegal cargo, and they were just as successful. He regained his strength from the good food,

Wages for a Smuggling Job

clean sea air, and regular exercise. But imprisonment had caused an unsual change in his body. As a young man at sea, Edmond had the sunburned face of a bronze god. But now, in spite of the hot Mediterranean sun, a permanent pallor marked his face.

Jacopo continued to be his friend, and Edmond taught him to handle the ship. The Italian was overjoyed by this, for such knowledge would enable him to rise above being just a deckhand. Jacopo often asked Edmond if he were not someone other than a mere sailor because he spoke and carried himself like a person of refinement. Edmond would only smile and not answer.

One night when they were on shore in Leghorn, the captain took Edmond to a tavern for a meeting with other smugglers. There, they were asked to take on a shipment of Turkish carpets, avoid paying duty, and transfer it to a ship bound for France. Some

A Meeting with Other Smugglers

deserted island would be selected where the cargo could be transferred in privacy.

The captain of the other boat leaned over the table and whispered, "Why don't we meet at the Island of Monte Cristo? It will be halfway for each of us."

Monte Cristo! Edmond's mouth went dry. The captains toasted their agreement for meeting on Monte Cristo with a glass of rum for all the smugglers. They did not notice that Edmond drank his with a shaking hand.

Edmond's boat arrived at Monte Cristo ahead of schedule, but his shipmates had no interest in going ashore. The island was uninhabited, rocky, and full of caves. Edmond announced that he would go ashore to try to shoot a wild goat for their dinner. Jacopo offered to go hunting with him, but Edmond put him in charge of building a fire on the beach to roast the meat.

Edmond walked quickly into the interior of

Monte Cristo in Sight!

the island and toward the caves. He never hesitated in his direction, for in his mind he saw Father Faria's map and heard the priest's instructions.

When he reached the mouth of the correct cave, he sat down and did nothing for a half-hour. He wanted to be sure he had not been followed for some innocent reason. When he was sure he was alone, he walked into the cave, his heart beating wildly. He concentrated . . . the back of the cave . . . the right stone moved . . . the corridor . . . the hidden spring . . . a door rolled back.

Edmond stepped into the dark room beyond. After fourteen years in his unlighted dungeon, Edmond had no trouble seeing in the dark. In a second he would know if the jailors had been right about Faria being a "mad priest." He looked around and gave a great sigh. Father Faria had not been mad!

Cardinal Spada's treasures lay before him.

Cardinal Spada's Treasures!

There were diamonds as large as eggs, rubies carved into roses, silver platters engraved with historical scenes, and piles and piles of gold bars. Four chests opened on emeralds and pearls fashioned into collars, necklaces of matching yellow diamonds, and other marvelously-worked pieces resting on layers of loose jewels that reached the halfway mark in each chest.

Edmond dared not stay long. He dipped his hand into one chest and poured a stream of flashing jewels into his handkerchief. He thrust the bundle inside his shirt and left. Outside he smothered his elation, saying very quietly, "Thank you, my dear friend and second father."

Then he hurried off to shoot a goat for the crew. Tomorrow would see the end of Edmond Dantes, smuggler. Tomorrow would see the beginning of Edmond Dantes, *avenger*!

A Stream of Flashing Jewels

Good-bye to a Smuggler's Life

CHAPTER 11

Caderousse Tells All

The smugglers welcomed the other boat to Monte Cristo, transferred their cargo of Turkish carpets, and received their usual pay—one hundred francs for each man. Edmond took his pay like the rest, but he smiled, for the smallest jewel in his handkerchief was worth ten times the entire payment to the crew.

When they anchored back in Leghorn, Edmond told the captain he would not ship out again. The captain offered to double his wages, but Edmond still refused, thanking him courteously. Seeing Jacopo's unhappy face, Edmond took him aside.

"My rescuer," he said, "I make you an offer. I need such a man as you—a man who is loyal and can hold his tongue. Will you come to work for me?"

Jacopo brightened instantly. "I would like nothing better. It is true, then, as I suspected, that you are not a sailor?"

"I sailed on this smuggling ship for amusement. But, yes, I am a sailor, among many other things. Now, get your belongings and wait for me in the town square."

Edmond went down a back street to the house of a dealer in precious stones and offered four small diamonds for sale. Though the dealer was accustomed to keeping an expressionless face, his eyes sparkled at the fine quality of the stones. He asked no questions as to how a poor sailor happened to own them. He gave Edmond forty thousand francs

Four Diamonds for Sale

and urged him to return any time he had more jewels to sell.

Edmond joined Jacopo in the town square. From that moment on, Jacopo's amazement grew. First Edmond ordered him to give all his belongings to the first beggar they met. Then he led Jacopo into the finest tailoring establishment in Leghorn. Here, Edmond ordered the doors to be shut to others and all the workers to concentrate on himself and Jacopo. At first the owner was indignant, but his eyes opened wide as Edmond tossed a thousand francs on a cutting table. He immediately ordered the doors closed.

Within an hour Edmond and Jacopo had been measured for a variety of outfits in the latest fashion and of the finest materials suitable for a gentleman and his personal servant. Edmond ordered them delivered to the Royal Hotel, the largest and fanciest hotel in Leghorn the following morning. The owner's

Measured for New Clothes

protests that this was an impossible demand
were cut short by a shower of more money.
As a result, he assured Edmond that his
tailors would work through the night without sleep.

Checking into the Royal Hotel proved no
more trouble than ordering their clothes.
Edmond's money got instant obedience to his
wishes from everyone. He was moved into a
set of rooms usually reserved for visiting
royalty. Jacopo hardly dared walk on the rugs
because they were so soft and beautiful.

Remembering all that Faria had taught him
about life among aristocrats, Edmond ordered
special dishes prepared and sent to his rooms,
along with the finest wines, fruits, and
cheeses.

When their clothes began to arrive the next
morning, Edmond gave his first important
order to Jacopo. He was to go to Marseilles
and, as inconspicuously as possible, he was to

Jacopo Hardly Dares Walk on the Rugs.

gather information on three people: old Monsieur Dantes, Mercedes, and Caderousse, their drunken neighbor. Jacopo left that afternoon with a purse full of money.

Edmond, himself, went to Genoa, where the shipbuilders excelled in trim, fast vessels. As his carriage drove past the bay, Edmond noticed a small yacht being tested. His keen eye appreciated how well the yacht handled, so he stopped and sought out the owner.

The owner, who was watching the tests sadly, was an Englishman. Many months ago he had ordered the yacht built to exacting specifications. Since then, he had lost money in speculations and could not afford to pay the balance due on the ship. Without hesitation, Edmond offered him the full price of the yacht plus twenty thousand francs beyond. The Englishman was delighted. He signed the yacht over to Edmond immediately.

Edmond found the yacht handled so well,

Edmond Notices a Small Yacht.

that with his experience he was able to sail her alone. He made one change—he had a closet installed in his bedroom aboard. It ran the length of one wall and from the outside, it appeared to be the wall itself.

After several trial runs, Edmond set course for Monte Cristo, but anchored first at a near-by island. He waited there a day to be sure he wasn't followed or seen by a passing ship. Then he moved the yacht to Monte Cristo and dropped anchor in a hidden cove. It took him two days to carry the Spada treasure from the cave and store it in his newly-made closet. He finished just in time to return to Leghorn to meet Jacopo.

Jacopo's news was bad. Edmond's father had died many years ago. Edmond had expected this, but still his heart turned over to hear it as a certainty. Mercedes had disappeared from Marseilles, and nothing was known about her. But Caderousse still lived

Moving the Treasure from Monte Cristo

there and owned a small roadside inn. Jacopo thought the inn must be a failure because the main road had shifted to another area, and no travelers went by. He gave Edmond the address, and Edmond set out for Marseilles immediately.

Jacopo had been right about the lack of travelers past Caderousse's inn. So it was a wonderful surprise to its owner and his wife to see a priest on a fine Hungarian horse coming down the road a few days later.

Long before the priest could hear him, Caderousse was calling, "Welcome, sir, a thousand welcomes!"

The priest stopped. The black of his clerical robe contrasted sharply with the pallor of his handsome face. When he asked for Caderousse by name, it was in a thick Italian accent.

"I am Gaspard Caderousse, Monsieur," replied the innkeeper, "and my inn is at your service."

A Priest Stops at Caderousse's Inn.

The priest ordered a bottle of Caderousse's best wine, then announced that he had come on a mission.

"I attended the deathbed of a prisoner named Edmond Dantes. He gave me a ring and asked me to sell it. He wanted the money divided among the five people closest to him in his youth, for he had come to think of them as his best friends. He named his father and you. He also named three men who I have not located yet: Danglars, Villefort, and a soldier named Fernand."

Caderousse's joy and wonder increased when the priest produced the ring—a huge ruby set in gold.

"But his father is dead," said Caderousse. "He died of starvation. Monsieur Morrel, who had been Edmond's friend and employer, found this out too late to save the old man who was too proud to beg. But Morrel paid for his funeral, and it was a fine one."

Old Monsieur Dantes Died of Starvation

Edmond. felt such pain at the news of his father's death by *starvation* that he had to remain quiet for a few moments. During the silence, a sly look came into Caderousse's eyes. He poured more wine for them both and then said in a decisive manner, "It is wrong that those other three men share in the inheritance. Monsieur Villefort was the Assistant Prosecutor for the King at that time, and it was he who imprisoned Dantes. Monsieur Morrel, the shipowner, and Mercedes, who was to be Dantes' wife, went often to Villefort to find what they could do to gain Dantes' release. He always refused to see them. Is that the action of a close friend? I say it is not!"

The priest nodded in agreement. "And the other two men?" he asked quietly. "What about them?"

Caderousse looked uncomfortable and took more wine to strengthen his resolve. Then he poured out the story of the letter which

Caderousse Tells His Story to the Priest.

Danglars had written with his left hand and which Fernand had mailed.

The priest looked at Caderousse severely. "This is a terrible story, if true. How can you know such a tale?"

Caderousse flushed. "I was there."

"What? You were there and permitted it to happen?" said the priest, shocked.

"Please, believe me, I hardly knew what was going on. I was drunk. I had no real part in it," babbled Caderousse.

The priest seemed to think it over. "I believe you, Caderousse. And since it is in my power to do as I believe Edmond Dantes would wish, I settle the entire inheritance on you alone." He gave Caderousse the ruby ring.

Caderousse almost fainted with joy. "Oh what have I done to deserve this good fortune. Maybe it is to make up for all the bad luck I've had in the past. Bless you, Edmond Dantes wherever you are!"

A Ruby Ring for Caderousse

The Talk of Paris Society

CHAPTER 12

The Count of Monte Cristo

Shortly after Edmond's visit to Caderousse, upper-class society in Paris was delighted to hear that an enormously rich and charming nobleman had settled in their city for a time. Since many titles were bought and not inherited, no one cared that this nobleman's family had never been heard of before. The Count of Monte Cristo had money and good manners, and Edmond knew these were enough.

After hearing Caderousse's confession, Edmond had decided to call himself the Count of Monte Cristo. He moved to Paris, sent

Jacopo on many errands to gather information, and began his war of revenge.

Edmond's first targets were Danglars and Villefort, co-owners of the largest bank in Paris. Danglars, always shrewd, had made a wartime fortune as a supervisor of supplies for the army. Though it was illegal for him to do so, he had purchased food and ammunition as a private merchant. Then as head of supplies for the army, he had bought his own goods for the government at an enormous price. He was now among the wealthiest men in Paris, but his passion was still to have more money. Since titles could be bought, he became known as Baron Danglars.

Villefort had become his associate, for he, too, always needed money. His connections with the government brought in international business and secret information. Though rich, Villefort had had some misfortunes personally. His first wife had died. His second

184

Baron Danglars, the Wealthy Banker

wife was highly nervous and terrified of poverty. They had been childless for many years, but now had a son, Edward, for whom both parents would gladly have died.

Villefort had come to the bank especially early one morning because Danglars wanted him to be present when he received the fabulously wealthy Count of Monte Cristo about whom all Paris was buzzing. Exactly on time the Count was announced and shown into Danglar's elaborate, antique-filled office.

Danglars was disturbed by his first sight of the tall, slender man with a pale, calm face. The Count's clothes were so fine, yet not showy, that Danglars felt shabby in his own rich garments. He did not like feeling inferior so he waved the Count in with a casual nod.

"Please come in, sir. No, it's 'Count,' isn't it? This is my associate, Monsieur Villefort. Sit down here. This chair once belonged to the Emperor of China. Now it belongs only to a

Villefort and His Family

baron." Danglars laughed nervously as he spoke.

Edmond nodded pleasantly to both men and handed Danglars a letter from the most famous bank in Rome, Thomson and French. Edmond had recently bought it but had ordered the purchase to remain a secret. Danglars read the letter with amazement.

"But it says here I am to give you *unlimited* credit while you are in Paris!"

"Yes," said Edmond, "that is the way I usually like things arranged."

"But *unlimited!* No, we must settle on a sum beyond which you cannot draw," decided Danglars. "That is only good business."

Edmond stood up. "Forgive me. I have been misinformed. I had been told yours was the largest bank in Paris, but I see you cannot meet my requirements."

Danglars and Villefort exchanged a look of surprise. Danglars said, "Now, wait, Count, of

The Count Wants *Unlimited* Credit.

course we can come to some agreement. Why don't we set the amount you can draw on at, say, one million francs? I'm sure you've never had such good treatment anyplace else."

Edmond was laughing. "Excuse my mirth, my dear Baron, but one million is ridiculous. I carry that amount with me all the time just in case I see some trinket I want to carry home with me." Edmond opened his money case and displayed more than the amount of money he had just claimed.

Danglars stared at it open-mouthed. Villefort left his chair so he, too, could see. The partners exchanged another quick look, and Danglars said, "You shall have any amount you desire, Count. Any amount!"

"Thank you, Baron Danglars. Also I may ask you to handle some investments for me from time to time. Perhaps I will buy some cargoes, cashmere or indigo from the East, you know. I will inform you what to buy... and,

"One Million Is Ridiculous."

most important, when to sell for me."

"Our bank is at your service," said Danglars and Villefort, almost together. The idea had come to them both at the same time that they could use the Count's instructions to invest on their own behalf.

From then on, there was constant communication between Danglars and Villefort's bank and the Count of Monte Cristo. Funds poured out of the bank for Edmond's new house, his carriage and matched gray horses, his large staff of servants, his entertainments, and his antiques and paintings.

Along with this activity Edmond sent a stream of orders to invest in numerous cargoes from all over the world. Danglars did as ordered, and each time he and Villefort invested some of their own money in the cargoes too. The first four investments returned such handsome profits that they were angry with themselves for not having risked more money.

The Count Buys a Carriage and Horses.

Soon both men had invested all their available money and were using the bank's assets for themselves. They had no fears of a loss.

When Edmond judged that Danglars and Villefort had overextended themselves financially, he came himself to the bank to order yet another investment—this time in a diamond mine. Edmond ordered three times his usual number of shares.

Danglars was amazed. "Dear Count," he said respectfully, "this must be a very important investment, since you have come in person to order it."

Edmond nodded solemnly. "It will make all my other investments seem unimportant. I expect to make huge sums."

As soon as Edmond left, Danglars signed notes for credit on all his belongings, including his four houses, his wife's inheritance, his daughter's dowry, and all their jewelry. Villefort, aware of his wife's intense desire to have

An Investment in a Diamond Mine

great wealth, hesitated. Then he reasoned that the success of this investment would make her ten times as secure as she was now, so he followed Danglars' example. The two men spent the next few weeks envisioning themselves the richest men in Paris, except for Monte Cristo.

During the next two months, reports of cargo shipments began to come in. Storms had wrecked ships. Cargoes had been captured by smugglers. And men who had once been trusted with transporting cash had vanished with it. Though somewhat disturbed by these reports, Danglars and Villefort remained happy and confident of their great wealth to come from the diamond mine.

Then the news came. The diamond mine was a fraud!

Danglars, pale and trembling, rushed to Monte Cristo's house. The Count was having a late breakfast and ordered coffee and fruit to

Danglars Discovers the Fraud!

be brought for Danglars.

Danglars gasped, "Count, how can you sit there so calmly and eat? We are ruined! The diamond mine was a fraud! "

Edmond smiled. "I heard a rumor some time ago that it might be. Through Thomson and French in Rome I sold my shares. I have lost nothing. This fruit is really excellent. Please try some."

Danglars sank down in a chair. "Why didn't you tell me. I am ruined, ruined!"

Edmond pretended surprise. "Oh, I didn't know you were investing in my choices. You have my sympathy. Jacopo, I will have more coffee."

Danglars rushed home. Without speaking to his family, he packed a suitcase with his clothes and his wife's jewelry. He raced to the bank and ordered all available cash brought to him. Neither the jewels nor money belonged to him, since he had already used both to gain

Ruined and Running Away

credit to invest in the mine. With this fortune Danglars fled from Paris.

When Villefort arrived at the bank, he found the employees in a turmoil. No one had given them instructions, but with no money available they had been forced to shut the doors of the bank. In Danglars' office Villefort found the report on the diamond mine. At this crushing blow, Villefort felt his mind waver. He fell into a chair and stared unseeing at the wall.

For five hours, no one could rouse Villefort until the butler from his house suddenly appeared and spoke to him. Villefort's wife had heard that something was wrong at the bank. Since her husband had not come home to tell her what the matter was, she had sent their butler for news. Remembering his wife and his beloved son, Edward, Villefort pulled himself together. He reminded himself that he still had his position with the government. Also he

A Crushing Blow for Villefort

determined to ask for his old position as Assistant Prosecutor again. Between the two, he could continue to support his family though, of course, not in their present high style. In time, he might be able to amass another fortune. Leaning on the butler's shoulder, Villefort made his way home.

Villefort went directly to his wife's room. She was in bed recovering from a nervous spell, but sat up trembling when her husband staggered in. Gently he told her what had happened and that they must move and make a new life. He promised her and their delicate Edward every care. He would work night and day to regain their lost position in life.

His wife seemed to take the news well. Villefort was still so shocked himself, he did not notice the terrible fear that suddenly flamed in her eyes. But she spoke calmly and asked that Edward be sent to her so she might have the pleasure of watching him at his lessons.

Villefort Breaks the News to His Wife.

Villefort left his wife and son together and went to lie down. A half-hour later he was awakened by the butler, who was weeping and holding out a note to Villefort.

In a trance Villefort read the note, in which his wife bade him good-bye and asked forgiveness. "I must take Edward where he will be safe forever. I know that security for him and me no longer lies in your house," she wrote.

Running to his wife's room, Villefort saw her slumped in death, cradling Edward, also dead, in her arms. She had poisoned herself and the boy.

At this sight, Villefort's mind snapped.

He began screaming and running about the room. He was so maddened that he did not notice the Count of Monte Cristo enter the room until he was standing beside him.

"You have ruined me," he shouted at Edmond. "You are the instrument of the devil."

Poisoned!

"No," replied Edmond solemnly. "I am the instrument of your own past evil. Look at me carefully, Villefort, and see if you can see a young, innocent sailor whom you betrayed with a smile and kind words!"

Villefort started back, putting out his hand to ward Edmond off. "It cannot be! No, you cannot be . . . . " He could not go on.

"Yes, I am Edmond Dantes," thundered Edmond, "and you deserve your fate."

Villefort started to groan and weep. "I admit it. I deserved it, but *they* did not!" He sank to his knees beside the bodies of his wife and son.

Now it was Edmond's turn to gasp. He bowed his head for a moment and murmured, "You are right. I had no hatred of them, only of you, Villefort."

Villefort looked up with a mad gleam in his eyes. "Not Villefort, Noirtier. Noirtier! Noirtier! Noirtier!" He chirped his father's name like

Villefort Goes Mad.

a bird, over and over.

A doctor had now arrived, and he shook his head sadly at Villefort, who was dancing and capering about the room.

"He is quite mad," said the doctor. "He must be bound or else he will hurt himself."

Edmond drove off with Villefort's screams and chirps trailing after his carriage. When he arrived home, he was greeted by Jacopo with the news that Danglars had been located.

"And as you ordered, sir, I had some of my old smuggling friends prepare a reception for him."

And they had. The smugglers had stopped Danglars' carriage along the road and dragged him from it, along with his precious suitcase. He was tossed into a bedroom in a farmhouse, but not harmed. At first Danglars was terrified, but he soon regained his confidence and demanded food and drink.

"Food has to be paid for here," said his

The Smugglers Kidnap Danglars.

guard. “Likewise, drink. Can you pay?”

“Of course, I can pay,” answered Danglars with scorn. “Bring me meat and wine.”

The man counted on his fingers. “That will cost ten thousand francs.”

For a moment Danglars was speechless. Then he cursed the man and announced he would rather starve than pay such a sum. He held out for two days and two nights until he got weak and thirsty. Then Danglars paid the ten thousand francs and was given a fine meal.

This pattern went on for a month. Soon Danglars was down to his last thousand francs. After a lifetime of greed, he could not bear the thought of being penniless. He held out for a week. Feeling close to death, Danglars realized his foolishness. Creeping to the door with his money in hand, he called weakly to the guard to bring water and food. But it wasn’t his guard who entered the room. It was a stranger whose face was hidden by his

Ten Thousand Francs for a Meal!

cloak.

"Do you suffer?" asked the stranger.

"Yes, I am starving," said Danglars.

"I know an old man who starved through your doing," said the man. "Do you repent?"

"I don't know who you mean, but yes, I repent, I repent," said Danglars weakly.

Edmond Dantes decided to show mercy because he was sorry for what had happened to Villefort's wife and son. He dropped his cloak. "I forgive you."

"The Count of Monte Cristo!" cried Danglars.

"No, Monsieur, I am Edmond Dantes."

Danglars gave a terrible gasp and fell backward. He trembled all over and wept.

Edmond looked at him with contempt and turned to the guard. "Feed him and let him go with his thousand francs. I want him out of my life forever."

Paris never heard of Baron Danglars again.

Edmond Dantes Forgives Danglars.

Albert Morcerf Admires a Fencer.

The Final Revenge

The young men of upper class in Paris spent several mornings each week taking fencing lessons. It was their ambition to hear a "Well done!" from the fencing master who was their hero.

Thus, young Albert Morcerf was amazed one day to see his fencing master hit three times in a row by his opponent's sword. When the match ended, Albert rushed over impulsively and congratulated the winner. The winner was amused at Albert's enthusiasm, and introduced himself as the Count of Monte

Cristo.

The two men formed a friendship, though they were so much apart in age. At home, Albert talked constantly of his new hero. His father, General Fernand Morcerf, was annoyed that his son should admire another man more than himself. But his mother, Mercedes, was delighted that such an elegant and educated man should befriend her son.

Albert invited the Count to tea to meet his parents. Even the general had to admit later that the Count was as witty and charming as all Paris had been claiming. But Mercedes, upon being introduced to the tall, handsome man, had grown faint and retired from the room.

As part of Edmond's plan for revenge, he had sent Jacopo to Constantinople, Turkey, to gather information about General Fernand Morcerf, who had served in the army there and who had returned to France with a fortune.

216

The Count Is Introduced to Mercedes.

Jacopo had also brought with him a young woman named Haydee—the daughter of the dethroned ruler, Ali Pasha. Haydee told the Count how she had been sold as a slave after her father had been betrayed and killed. She accused General Morcerf, who had once been her father's friend, of the murder.

Edmond saw to it that these accusations appeared in the newspapers and that a Committee of Inquiry was formed. General Morcerf was forced to appear and hear the testimony of the daughter of Ali Pasha.

Albert, horrified at the scandal, learned through friends one night that the man responsible for bringing this information to the courts was the Count of Monte Cristo.

Half-crazed, Albert rushed through Paris looking for him. Then he discovered that Edmond was at the opera that night. Albert burst into the theater and noisily entered Edmond's box. Before the whole audience he

Haydee Accuses General Morcerf of Murder.

challenged the Count of Monte Cristo to a duel.

Edmond nodded coldly. "It will be my pleasure, Monsier Morcerf. Now, please withdraw, for my favorite aria is about to be sung."

When Edmond returned from the opera, Jacopo said, "Sir, a lady has insisted on waiting for you. She would not leave."

Edmond entered his parlor and found Madame Mercedes Morcerf, Albert's mother waiting, her lovely face stained with tears. Edmond bowed politely. But she threw herself at his feet and pleaded, "Edmond, do not kill my son."

Edmond's head jerked up. "What name do you call me by, Madame Morcerf?"

Mercedes came closer. "Do you think I could mistake you, Edmond? When you walked into my house that first time with Albert, I knew at once you were Edmond Dantes. In my heart

Albert Challenges the Count to a Duel.

I knew you."

Edmond laughed harshly. "Yes, that heart, Mercedes. A heart that was first mine, then given to Fernand."

"But I was desperate and lonely after you disappeared, Edmond," she cried. "I waited for years. I worked with Monsieur Morrel for your release. Fernand was the only friend I had left after your father died."

"And do you know why I disappeared?" Edmond asked scornfully.

"Why, you were arrested and imprisioned."

"Yes," replied Edmond, and then he began the tale of his fourteen years in the Chateau d'If. As he talked, the pain on Mercedes' face increased. When he finished, she sat with bowed head as if struck by a club. With an effort she finally spoke.

"You have suffered terribly. But was it necessary to expose Fernand's betrayal of Ali Pasha just because he married me?"

"I Waited for Years."

Edmond's eyes were fierce. "No, Mercedes. I have exposed him because he betrayed me. He was the cause of my imprisonment."

Mercedes' horror increased as she heard the story of the accusing letter sent by her husband.

"I understand your need for vengeance, Edmond. But you are planning to duel my son. Why must this vengeance fall on the son as well as the father?"

"I never intended to involve Albert," he replied sadly. "The young man's hot blood did that. But I will do as you ask. I will spare your son's life. But in doing so, I must die!"

"Die? What are you saying?"

Edmond sighed. "I will go to the duel and fire my pistol into the air. Your son, whose skill at guns I myself have been improving with lessons, will fire at my heart. I have no doubt his bullet will find its home. Ah, Mercedes, my life is about to end for the second time. The

"I Will Spare Your Son's Life."

first time was when your husband put me in prison. This time it will be because of your son's bullet."

Mercedes could only murmur through her tears, "Bless you, Edmond. I was sure that the heart of the young Edmond I once knew could not have changed so much that it would willingly sacrifice an innocent boy. Thank you, my dear, and farewell."

After Mercedes left, Edmond sat for a long while thinking about the past and his plans for revenge—plans he must now give up because he had not counted on one factor—his love for Mecercedes. And he thought about the future—a future that would no longer exist for him after this day.

When Edmond appeared at the secluded space in the forest chosen for the duel, Albert's seconds, or witnesses, were filled with anxiety. Albert had not been at home when they called, and they feared he had gone to the court to

"Bless You, Edmond."

hear the verdict in his father's case. All knew there could be only one verdict after the testimony of Ali Pasha's daughter. In actually hearing his father condemned for treason, Albert might be too upset to aim his pistol carefully.

Their relief was great when a carriage clattered up and Albert rushed from it, calling to his friends, "I must speak to the Count of Monte Cristo, and I want you all to hear what I have to say."

Edmond stood waiting calmly as Albert and his amazed friends approached.

Albert bowed formally and said, "Sir, my quarrel with you did not concern itself with the guilt or innocence of my father in his actions toward Ali Pasha. My anger was in your bringing the matter to the attention of the courts. As you will soon hear, my father has been found guilty of felony, treason, and dishonor." Albert's voice did not falter as he said

Edmond Awaits Albert's Arrival.

these terrible words.

He continued, "However, sir, I have now heard of an even more wicked action by this same general—I no longer wish to call him 'father.' It is a betrayal of an innocent young sailor, whose subsequent suffering cannot be spoken of without tears. The reason for this duel is now meaningless when compared to this betrayal. Oh, how I wish I could repay you for your years of suffering. As it is, all I can do is humbly beg your pardon, Count."

Albert extended his hand, and Edmond took it with his head bowed. He realized that after he had offered Mercedes *his* life, this courageous woman had saved it by confessing a terrible family secret to her son, even though she risked losing his love by doing so.

Albert then took Edmond's arm, and they moved away from the others.

"My mother also told me that you and she were once pledged to one another," said Albert.

"I Humbly Beg Your Pardon, Count."

"I can only wish that your lives had not been separated. Then I might have had a father I could be proud of."

There were tears in Edmond's eyes as he drove home. Jacopo, looking nervous and worried, met him on the entrance steps.

"General Morcerf is here, sir. The news about the duel has already reached him. In fact, half of Paris knows of the apology by now."

Edmond did not hurry or slow his step, though his final revenge was at hand. He greeted Fernand coolly and offered him refreshment. But Fernand was in a rage, with blood throbbing visibly at his temples. He whirled to face Edmond.

"What have I done to you that you have ruined my life? Is this some favorite sport of yours to search out a man's past mistakes and punish him for them? And then to add to my humiliation, my son turns against me and

Fernand Is in a Rage.

apologizes to my enemy. What is this power you have? . . . And why me?"

Edmond sat down and said calmly, "Oh, you are not the only one, Fernand. The other two I have ruined were Danglars and Villefort. They are your associates, I believe?"

Suddenly Fernand recognized the voice and made the connection between himself and the men mentioned. He shrank back and uttered a piercing cry, "No! It cannot be! No, Edmond Dantes is dead!" Then he collapsed.

As Edmond turned to leave the room, he looked back at the motionless figure on the floor and cried, "Not dead, but here before you. The Count of Monte Cristo has cut off your life as you cut off Edmond Dantes' life."

When Fernand came to, he was alone. He staggered to his carriage and made his way home. He was about to pull up at his door when he saw Mercedes and Albert hurrying down the steps, carrying two small suitcases.

Mercedes and Albert Leave Home.

THE COUNT OF MONTE CRISTO

A public carriage drew up, and Albert helped his mother into it.

"Do not look back, Mother," he said. "This is no longer our home. Soon you will be back in Marseilles, in the house where you were happy as a girl. And I shall be off to sea to seek my fortune."

As the carriage rounded the corner, a shot rang out in the garden of the Morcerf house. General Fernand Morcerf had killed himself. The Count of Monte Cristo had taken revenge on the enemies of Edmond Dantes!

Sometime that same night, the Count of Monte Cristo boarded his yacht to embark on a voyage alone. Jacopo shook his hand and tearfully asked, "Will we ever meet again?"

"My friend," said Edmond, "only God knows what the future will bring. And until He decides to reveal that future to man, man must simply wait and hope . . . as I did for so many years . . . wait and hope."

" `. . . Wait and Hope."